CHARLEY
the Bulldog's
FANTASTIC FRUIT STAND

written by
ANDY FRISELLA

illustrated by KEVIN CANNON
created by Andy Frisella and Vaughn Kohler

WISE INK

ISBN 13: 978-1-63489-050-2

Library of Congress Catalog Number: 2016954271

Printed in the United States of America
Fourth Printing: 2022

26 25 24 23 22   8 7 6 5 4

Cover and interior illustration and design by Kevin Cannon
Story co-created by Vaughn Kohler

Wise Ink Creative Publishing
807 Broadway St. NE, Suite 46
Minneapolis, MN 55413
wiseink.com

To order, visit OtisandCharley.com or contact Itasca Books at 1-800-901-3480 (itascabooks.com).
Reseller discounts available.

★ About Otis & Charley ★

This is a story about Otis and Charley, two funny and friendly bulldogs who live on a great big farm with their mom and dad. Their dad is a big man with a beard who loves to drive fast cars. Their mom is a nice lady with blonde hair who likes to cook.

Otis likes to laugh and lie around doing nothing. Charley is sweet, smart, and always stays busy.

Sometimes they don't get along, but most of the time they have great fun together. They are always learning how having big dreams and working hard can make you happy.

OTIS   CHARLEY

"Hey, Charley!" said Otis, sitting in his favorite spot in front of the television. "What are you doing?"

"I'm writing plans for what I need to do today," Charley said. Charley was one of the few bulldogs in history who could read and write. (Do you believe that?)

"I am going to open a fantastic fruit stand!"

"Open a fruit stand? What does that mean?"
Otis asked, scratching his head.

"I am going to sell fruit to the people who come by our farm," Charley said.

"First, Mom is going to take me to the store. I will buy apples, bananas, pears, and maybe a big green watermelon.

Then, Dad is going to help me build a stand so I can sell the fruit."

Otis giggled. "You're crazy! That doesn't sound fun at all. That sounds like a lot of hard work!"

"It is hard work," said Charley. "But hard work can make you really happy!"

Otis looked back at the television and
cocked his head. How could hard work be fun?
Watching television was perfect fun for Otis!

"Right now, I have to get my tail moving!" Charley said.

"Whatever," Otis said. "I'm just going to stay here and sit on my tail."

Otis sat on his tail all morning and watched
The Dogs of Our Lives on Pupapalooza TV.

Meanwhile, Charley went to the store.

She sat in the cart and picked out big red apples, bright yellow bananas, speckled pears, and even a big green watermelon.

At lunchtime, Otis ate his food in
front of the television, sitting on his tail.

Charley ate lunch, too, but then she went to the barn with her dad. They took some wood and tools and built a stand and a sign that read, "Charley's Fantastic Fruit Stand."

It was hard work.

In the afternoon, Otis was still watching television...

...and sitting on his tail, of course!

"Yawn!" said Otis. "It sure is tiring sitting on my tail!"

Otis wasn't really tired—he was just bored. Not to mention, Otis's tail had been numb since lunch!

(Has that ever happened to you?)

Outside, Charley set up her fruit stand. It was very, very hot outside. At first, no one came by. But Charley did not give up!

Then finally . . . one customer!

Then two more customers . . .

Then *five* more customers!

Later that evening, Otis finally turned off the television, but he kept sitting on his tail. "Boy, oh boy," he said.

"This day was boring. Nothing exciting happened."

Just then, Charley came in with a new toy—
the coolest, neatest, most special toy that
Otis had ever seen. "Hi, Otis!" Charley said.

"Wow!" Otis said.
"That's the coolest, neatest,
best toy I've ever seen! Did
Mom and Dad buy that for you?
Did they buy one for me, too?"

fun!

"Sorry, Otis. This is the only one. I bought it myself," Charley said.

"How?" Otis said. "That toy looks expensive! And you're just a bulldog!"

"I earned money at my fruit stand," Charley said. "I worked hard. I sold a lot of fruit. I saved most of my money. But with a little bit of it, I bought this toy."

"You know, it was fun to buy the toy, but the best part of my day was selling the fruit at my fantastic fruit stand. Working hard to build something special makes me happy," Charley said.

"Holy moly!" said Otis. "I think I would like to work hard, too, so I can be happy like you."

"Otis, you can play with my toy," said Charley.
"But you have to promise me something."

"Yes!" said Otis. "Anything!"

"Tomorrow, I'm going to sell
some more fruit at my fantastic
fruit stand," Charley said.
"Will you promise to help?"

"Yeah! Yeah, yeah, yeah!
I promise!" said Otis.

That evening, Charley and Otis played together with Charley's new toy. Then they sat on their tails for a while, but not to watch television . . .

...as they sat, they talked and laughed as they planned all the adventures and hard work for the next day.

About the Author

When he's not creating books for kids, **ANDY FRISELLA** is the CEO of 1st Phorm International, a sport performance/nutritional supplement company based in St. Louis, Missouri. (Basically, they help people win in sports and life.) A highly sought-after speaker and consultant, Andy is what adults call "the industry-leading expert at customer loyalty, creating fanatical culture, and building brick-and-mortar as well as direct-to-consumer retail businesses."

Growing up, Andy learned life-changing lessons from his dad and mom. (He also learned a ton from the challenge of building a nine-figure business!) For this reason, he wanted to teach fundamental principles of happiness and success to boys and girls who were still young—so the lessons would make the most impact! That's why he created Otis & Charley's Hardworking Tails. Of course, parents (and other adults) can also learn how to be successful in business and life by listening to Andy's popular podcast series, *Real AF with Andy Frisella*, and by reading his bestselling book on mental toughness, *75Hard: A Tactical Guide to Winning the War with Yourself*. Find these resources (and more!) at:

andyfrisella.com

About the Co-Creator

VAUGHN KOHLER

Vaughn Kohler is a writer, editor, speaker, and consultant. He has served as a cohost and frequent contributor on both of Andy Frisella's top-rated business and success podcasts. Sharing his

friend's love for dogs and hard work, Vaughn helps Andy generate story ideas and provides editorial feedback. He and his wife, Kasia, live in Manhattan, Kansas, with their four daughters. Find him online at:

vaughnkohler.com

About the Illustrator

KEVIN CANNON

can usually be found pulling twelve-hour shifts doing what he loves most: illustrating children's books, drawing graphic novels, or creating cartoon maps. Over the years, Cannon has cofounded a few small businesses, including an award-winning art studio, an animation studio, and a short-lived (but still very fun) tech start-up. He lives in Minneapolis, Minnesota.

kevincannon.org

Did you enjoy
Charley the Bulldog's Fantastic Fruit Stand?
Have we got great news for you! There are
more Otis & Charley stories available!

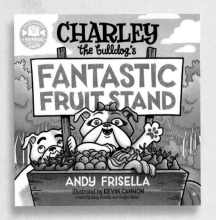

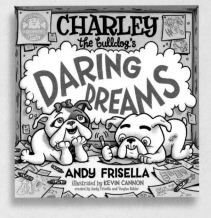

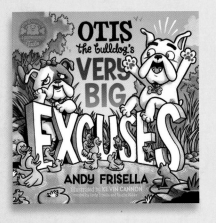

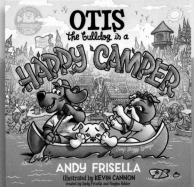

OTIS and CHARLEY.com